Disney
Winnie the Pooh

It's Fun to Learn

Blow, Wind, Blow

One blustery day in the Hundred-Acre Wood, Kanga was helping Roo get ready for the autumn Kite-Flying Festival. Everyone made a special kite to fly in the festival to welcome fall.

"My stripedy kite will fly tiggerifically high!" said Tigger.

"Ha!" said Rabbit. "Not as high as my sturdy carrot kite."

"My kite may look like a book," said Owl, "but she's as light as a feather!"

"And my kite is the color of trees," added Roo proudly.

"Oh, bother," said Pooh. "My kite is the stickiest. It must have been that smackerel of honey I had for breakfast."

"Sorry, Eeyore," said Rabbit, shaking his head. "You're going to have to fix your kite before you can be in the festival. It's gone and lost its tail, just like you."

"Look, Eeyore!" called Roo, waving something in the air. "I found your kite's missing tail."

"Gee, thanks," said Eeyore. "But I'll probably just lose it again."

When it was time for the festival, the wind had died down to a whisper.

"Oh, dear," said Kanga. "I'm afraid we've lost our windy day."

"Wait, Mama," cried Roo. "I'm running as fast as I can to get my kite up in the air!"

"This is ridickerous," Tigger complained. "I can't even bounce my kite up there. And bouncin' is what tiggers do best."

Poor Owl tried to get a flying start with his kite, but he ended up getting tangled in a tree branch.

Everyone was very disappointed.

"Well," said Kanga, "the wind, just like other things in nature, is unpredictable."

"What does that mean, Mama?" asked Roo.

"Just this, Roo," she explained. "Listen carefully:

So very often the wind comes and goes.

It whispers when calm, and howls when it blows."

"Oh, my," said Pooh thoughtfully. "Since the wind comes and goes so quickly, maybe the sun does, too. I better go get my umbrella just in case it rains."

"Let's meet back here for the Kite-Flying Festival when the wind starts up again," said Kanga.

"Mama," called Roo, "is it okay if I go get my boat to sail on the pond?"

"Yes, dear," said Kanga, "as long as you're careful and bring a friend to watch you."

"I'll come with you, Roo," said Piglet, "and look for haycorns."

"Well, it's back to planting for me," said Rabbit, hurrying off to his garden.

"Watch this, Buddy Boys!" cried Tigger. "I spy some leaves just waitin' to get bounced!"

While Tigger was busy bouncing, Owl headed home to pull the leaves out of his feathers.

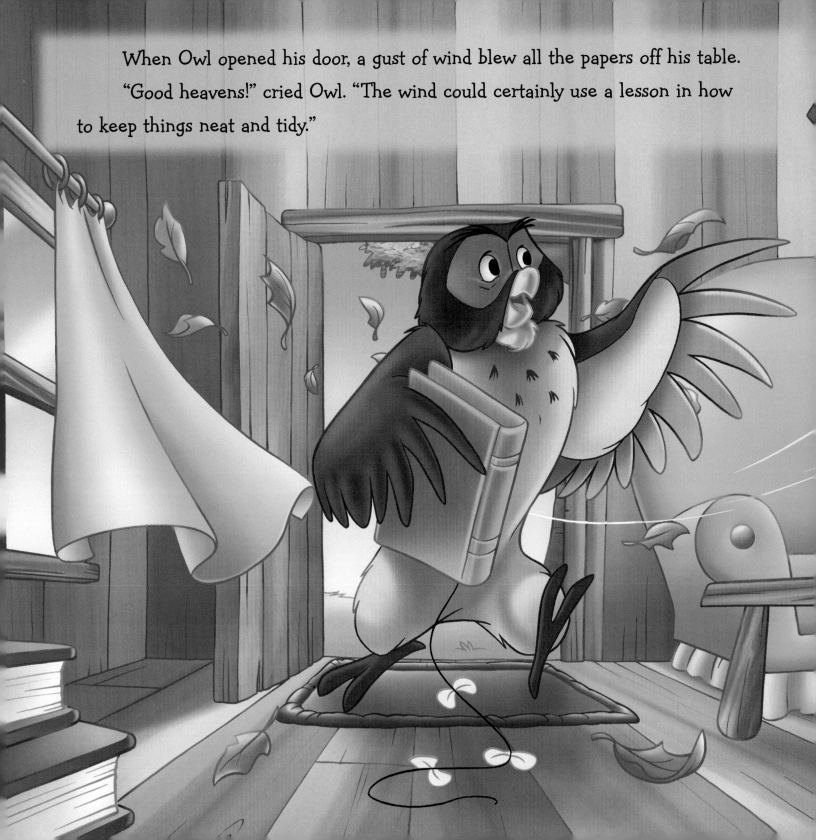

When Owl opened his door, a gust of wind blew all the papers off his table. "Good heavens!" cried Owl. "The wind could certainly use a lesson in how to keep things neat and tidy."

Back at home, Kanga was looking for her apron.

Suddenly it blew in off the clothesline and landed right on her head.

"Well," said Kanga, "I better take my laundry in before the wind does it for me."

Suddenly another gust of wind blew through the Wood. Roo watched his
boat *whoosh* across the stream.

"Gee," said Roo, "the wind is not only making my boat move, it's making the
water move, too!"

"Oh, dear," said Piglet. "The wind has changed its mind again."

Meanwhile, Pooh had just headed out the door with his umbrella to join Piglet and Roo when he suddenly got caught up in the wind.

"Bother," thought Pooh, pushing back the breeze with all his might. "What a pushy sort of wind."

In Rabbit's garden, his weather vane was spinning madly in the breeze.

"The Kite-Flying Festival!" cried Rabbit. "If the wind is back, it must be starting. I better hurry."

Rabbit rushed out of his garden and went to find Eeyore.

But when he got to Eeyore's, the wind had knocked down his house of sticks.

"Come on, Eeyore!" cried Rabbit. "Let's catch this wind while we can. We'll rebuild your house later! And don't forget your kite tail!"

Tigger noticed that the leaves on the ground were now swirling all around him.

He even got some help bouncing from the wind.

"Hoo-hoo-hoo!" he cried. "What a ride! Blow, wind, blow!"

When he got to the festival, he saw his friends holding tightly onto their kites.

"Hurry!" cried Roo. "We don't want the wind to change its mind again."

"You're right," said Kanga. "On your mark, get set, fly!"

And before Tigger could say "what a wunnerful wind," a great big *whoosh* lifted the friends right off the ground and carried them up into the air with the kites.

"Wow!" cried Tigger. "Now, that's what I call some high-flyin' pals!"

Fun to Learn Activity

Hello, dears. Wasn't that a windy little tale? The wind kept changing its mind that day in the Hundred-Acre Wood. See if you can go back and find all the different things the wind did in the story.

On the next windy day that blows your way, look and listen outside and observe what the wind does! What happens to the grass, leaves, and trees around you?